D1444899

For Nicola, Eliza, Jack and Tom
~A.M.

For Miles, with love
~J.M.

This edition published by Scholastic Inc; 557 Broadway; New York, NY 10012,
by arrangement with Little Tiger Press. SCHOLASTIC and associated logos
are trademarks and/or registered trademarks of Scholastic Inc
Scholastic Canada; Markham, Ontario

International Standard Book Number: 1-84506-436-4

Text copyright © Anne Mangan 1995
Illustrations copyright © Joanne Moss 1995

Original edition published in English by Little Tiger Press,
an imprint of Magi Publications, London, England, 1995.

This edition copyright © Good Books, Intercourse, PA 17534, 2005

Library of Congress Cataloging-in-Publication Data is available for this title.

All rights reserved. No part of this book may be reproduced in any manner,
except for brief quotations in critical articles or reviews, without permission.

Printed in China

Little Teddy Left Behind

Anne Mangan   Joanne Moss

Good Books®

Intercourse, PA 17534
800/762-7171
www.GoodBks.com

Little Teddy woke up and sneezed loudly. Nobody heard him because there was no one there. Nicole and Jack had moved to a new house.

"I'm all alone," said Teddy. "They've left me behind. They never were very good at packing." It was so dusty that he sneezed again. "Achoo!"

It grew dark, and at last Teddy went to sleep again.

The next morning the cleaning woman's
dog spotted him and picked him up.
"What do you have there?" asked the
woman. When she saw how grubby Teddy was,
she grabbed him with her big hands . . .

. . . and popped him into the washing machine!

"Oh, help!" cried Little Teddy, but she didn't hear his tiny squeak.

It was terrible in the washing machine. Teddy whirled around and around until he was quite dizzy. He growled his very loudest growl, but nobody came to rescue him.

At last he was spun dry, and the machine stopped. Teddy lay there among all the damp clothes, wondering what would happen next.

The cleaning woman opened the washing machine door and took him out. "You're not quite dry yet," she said.

"I am so!" growled Little Teddy, but she didn't seem to hear. In a moment she'd pinned him upside down on the clothesline.

"I'd rather be dirty and right side up!" he cried.

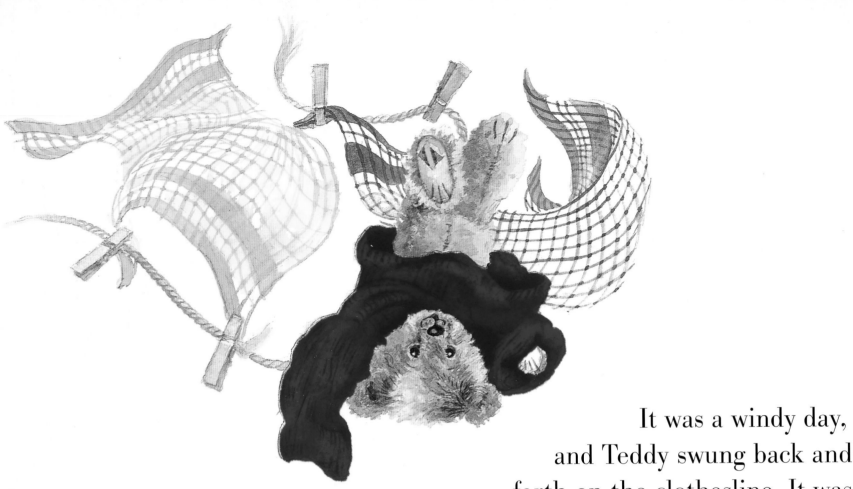

It was a windy day,
and Teddy swung back and
forth on the clothesline. It was
exciting in a way, like flying in space.
All at once the line broke, and Teddy fell down, down, down.
"It's a good thing bears have so much fluff," he thought as he
landed in the grass. Butterflies flew around him, and bees buzzed
over his head. Little Teddy liked the bright, cheerful butterflies,
but he was afraid of the bees.

"You scare me," he squeaked, even though they were
too busy to hear him.

Suddenly Teddy felt hot breath in his ear.

"Oh no!" he cried. "It's that dog again!"

The dog seized Little Teddy in his big teeth and
pushed through a very prickly hedge into the next yard.

"Oh, my poor fur!" gasped Teddy.

A woman looked up as the dog rushed onto her lawn.
"Ugh, you've got a rat in your mouth!" she screamed,
throwing her garden glove at them.

"I'm not a rat!" growled Teddy.

The dog ran out through
the garden gate into the woods.
"I wish he'd drop me," thought poor Teddy. Finally,
the dog spotted a rabbit and ran off, leaving Teddy behind.
Teddy lay very still, hoping the dog wouldn't come back.
It was quiet in the woods—but not for long. A boy and a girl
came rushing toward him.
"Hey, a little teddy!" cried the boy, picking him up.

"Catch!" he shouted, and poor
Teddy was tossed from one to the other until he
felt quite sick. Jack and Nicole had never played
with him like this.

At last the children grew tired of their game,
and the girl flung Little Teddy high into the air.

Up, up, up he sailed, right into the branches
of a tall tree. No sooner had he landed than he
heard an angry chattering noise.

"Trying to steal my nuts, are you?"

Teddy looked down from his perch. On the next branch a squirrel was glaring at him. Teddy tried to explain about the boy and girl and their awful game of catch, but the squirrel didn't seem to hear. "This is my tree!" he said, giving Teddy a sudden push. The little bear fell down, down, down . . .

. . . and landed on a wooden floor.

He was still catching his breath and
wondering how Jack and Nicole would
ever find him, when he heard children's voices.
He tried his growl and he tried his squeak,
but they were too small for anyone to hear him.

The floor was as dusty as the empty room
he had left behind. Once again Little Teddy
began to sneeze and sneeze. The sneezes were
louder than the growls and squeaks, and soon
the voices came nearer . . .

"Look, there's a ladder!"

"It's a tree house!"

Two faces were peering at him—two faces he knew very well!

"It's Little Teddy!" cried Jack. "How did he get into our new yard? I thought he was still packed up."

"I don't know," said Nicole, giving Teddy a hug. "Maybe he's been exploring his new home. What a wonderful tree house he's found!"

"Let's call it the Teddy House," said Jack.

His very own house! Little Teddy liked the idea.

A few days later, Nicole and Jack had
a housewarming party for all their friends. And each
friend brought a teddy bear, so that Little Teddy could
have his *own* party in his new home in the big tree.